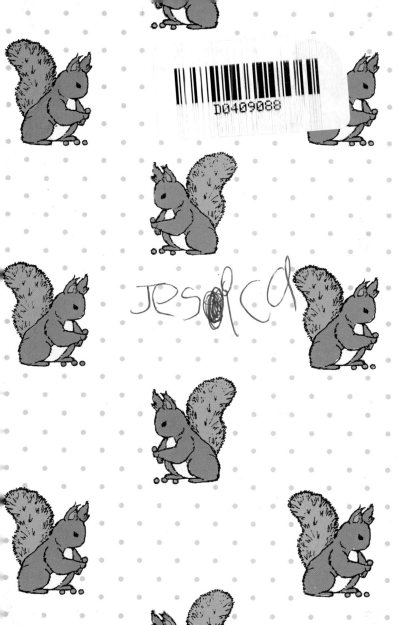

JESSICA

Acknowledgments
Designed by Liz Antill. Photographs by Tim Clark and art direction by Roy Smith. Models made by Stan and Vera Veasey of Technique and backgrounds illustrated by John Berry.

British Library Cataloguing in Publication Data

Hately, David
    Beatrix Potter's The tale of Squirrel Nutkin.
    —(Beatrix Potter series no. 876).
    I. Title   II. Potter, Beatrix. Tale of Squirrel Nutkin
    823'.914[J]   PZ7
    ISBN 0-7214-1020-0

First edition

Published by Ladybird Books Ltd Loughborough Leicestershire UK
Ladybird Books Inc Lewiston Maine 04240 USA

Text and illustrations copyright © Frederick Warne & Co., MCMLXXXVII
Based on *The Tale of Squirrel Nutkin* by Beatrix Potter
copyright © Frederick Warne & Co., MCMIII
© In presentation LADYBIRD BOOKS LTD MCMLXXXVII

All rights reserved. No part of this publication may be reproduced, stored in a retrieval system, or transmitted in any form or by any means, electronic, mechanical, photo-copying, recording or otherwise, without the prior consent of the copyright owners.

Printed in England

The tale of Squirrel Nutkin

Based on the original and authorised story
by **Beatrix Potter**

adapted by David Hately

Ladybird Books
in association with Frederick Warne

This is the story of a red squirrel called Nutkin, and what happened to his tail.

Nutkin and his brother Twinkleberry,

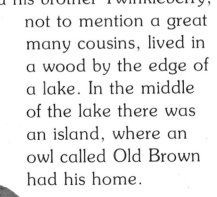

not to mention a great many cousins, lived in a wood by the edge of a lake. In the middle of the lake there was an island, where an owl called Old Brown had his home.

Old Brown's island was covered with beautiful nut trees. One autumn day, when the nuts were ripe for gathering, the squirrels made rafts out of twigs. Then they each took a sack and a raft and, using their bushy tails to act as sails, they paddled across to Old Brown's island.

The squirrels took three fat mice with them as a present for Old Brown. They put the mice on the doorstep and knocked at the door.

Old Brown came to the door to see who was there, and all the squirrels bowed politely. 'Good day, Mr Brown,' said Twinkleberry. 'Please may we gather some nuts from your trees? We have to stock up ready for the winter.'

Old Brown examined the three fat mice. They looked very tasty, so he gave the squirrels a gracious nod. Off they went to fill up their sacks with nuts.

But Squirrel Nutkin did not go with them. He danced about in front of Old Brown, bobbing up and down like a little red **cherry** and singing a riddle,

Riddle-me, riddle-me, rot-tot-tote!
A little wee man in a red, red coat!

Old Brown took no notice. Indeed, he shut his eyes and went to sleep. So Nutkin went off to play, leaving his brother and his cousins to fill up the sacks by themselves.

That evening, they all sailed home with their sacks full of nuts for their winter store cupboards.

Next day, the squirrels returned to the island. This time they brought with them a fine fat mole as a present for Old Brown. Again he gave them permission to gather nuts. He eyed the fine fat mole for a moment, then fell fast asleep.

But this time Squirrel Nutkin took a **stinging nettle**, and

he tickled Mr Brown with it, singing,

Old Mr B! Riddle-me-ree!
If you touch Hitty Pitty,
Hitty Pitty will bite you!

Mr Brown woke up suddenly, and gave Squirrel Nutkin a look. Then he went into his house, taking the fine fat mole with him.

Old Brown made a fire in the grate so that he could cook his supper. Nutkin watched as a thread of blue **smoke** came up out of the chimney in the owl's tree. Then Nutkin peeped through the keyhole and began to sing at the top of his voice,

A house full, a hole full,
And you cannot gather a bowl full!

Again Old Brown took no notice of Squirrel Nutkin, who soon grew tired of singing.

The other squirrels were still busy searching for nuts, but Nutkin gathered some yellow and scarlet oakapples and played marbles with them outside Old Brown's front door.

On the third day, which was Wednesday, all the squirrels (except Nutkin) got up bright and early. They went fishing and caught seven fat minnows as a present for Old Brown. Nutkin got up just in time to join them as they paddled across to the island.

When the squirrels landed, Nutkin raced ahead because he had thought of another riddle to tease Mr Brown.

But Old Brown was still not interested in riddles.

On the fourth day the squirrels brought six fat black beetles for Mr Brown. Each beetle was wrapped up in a dock leaf and fastened with a pin made from a pine needle.

Old Brown was pleased with the beetles, which were as delicious to him as the plums in **plum pudding** are to you and me.

But Nutkin still showed no respect. He sang rudely,

Old Mr B! Riddle-me-ree!
Flour and fruit from a Spanish tree,
Put in a bag, tied round with a string,
If you tell me this riddle,
I'll give you a ring!

Of course, Nutkin did not have a ring to give. Old Brown merely gave Nutkin another look, and went inside with the fat black beetles.

Twinkleberry and the other squirrels hunted for more nuts, but Nutkin spent the day collecting robins' pincushions from a briar bush and sticking them full of pine needle pins.

On the fifth day the squirrels
brought Old Brown a present of
wild honey that they had gathered
from the nest of some **bumble bees**.

The other squirrels went off in
search of more nuts but Nutkin
stayed outside Old Brown's
front door, skipping up and

down, and singing,

> *Hum-a-bum! Buzz! Buzz!*
> *Hum-a-bum buzz!*
> *The handsomest pigs striped yellow*
> *and black,*
> *All in a flock with wings on*
> *their backs!*

Old Brown ignored the rude little squirrel and Nutkin spent the rest of the day playing skittles with a crab apple and some green fir cones.

On the sixth day, which was Saturday, the squirrels came to the island for the last time. As a special farewell present they brought Old Brown a new laid **egg**. But Nutkin ran about singing,

Humpty Dumpty sat on the wall,
Humpty Dumpty had a great fall.

Old Brown wasn't a bit interested, but he *was* interested in the egg. He picked it up and took it inside.

Nutkin tried harder than ever to tease Old Brown. He danced about like a **sunbeam**, singing,

Old Mr B! Old Mr B!
All the king's horses and all
*   the king's men couldn't move me*
From the kitchen wall.

Nutkin peered in through Old Brown's window. The owl saw him, and this time the look he gave the squirrel was almost a glare.

When Twinkleberry and the others came back in the evening to say thank you and goodbye to Old Brown, Nutkin suddenly took a run and a jump at the owl's head!

Then Nutkin made a whirring noise to sound like the **wind**, and he began to sing,

*I come roaming up the land
But you can't hold me in your hand.
The King of Scotland, though he might try,
Couldn't stop me as I rush by!*

All of a sudden there was a flutter. Then there was a scutter. Finally there was a loud *squeak!*

The squirrels dived for cover and, when at last they peeped out from their hiding places, there was Old Brown sitting by his front door, as though nothing had happened.

But Nutkin was tucked inside his waistcoat pocket!

You may think that this is the end of the story, but it isn't.

Old Brown went inside his house and held Nutkin up by the tail, intending to skin him.

But Nutkin struggled and struggled so hard that his tail broke in two!

Nutkin dashed up the staircase and escaped through an attic window high up in the tree house.

He ran as fast as he could through the wood and raced back to the shore of the lake.

And to this day, if you meet Squirrel Nutkin up a tree and ask him a riddle, do you know what will happen? Nutkin will throw sticks at you, and stamp his feet, and scold and shout, *'Cuck-cuck-cuck-cur-r-r-uck-k-k!'*

For Squirrel Nutkin has hated riddles ever since the day when Old Brown left him with only half a tail. And he was lucky to get away with *that*, don't you think?